Vivaldi's Ring of Mystery

text by
Douglas Cowling

art by
Laura Fernandez & Rick Jacobson

North Winds Press
A Division of Scholastic Canada Ltd.

The illustrations for this book were painted in oils on canvas.

This book was typeset in 14 point Galliard.

Author's note:
History is full of people whose voices are not heard and whose words were never written down:
women, slaves — and children. The story of Vivaldi can be told because he was an important
historical figure whose manuscripts, records and letters were saved. Because of this,
we know much about his daily life, how he worked and even that he had red hair.

But we have no letters or records from the hundreds of children he taught and
to whose lives he gave meaning and beauty. We must use our imagination
to hear their hopes and fears, their loneliness and their laughter.
While the existence of the Pietà and its orphaned student musicians
are a part of recorded history, our plot and dialogue are fictional.

National Library of Canada Cataloguing in Publication

Cowling, Douglas
Vivaldi's ring of mystery / Douglas Cowling;
illustrated by Laura Fernandez & Rick Jacobson.
Based on musical CD for children.
ISBN 0-439-96904-2

1. Vivaldi, Antonio, 1678-1741—Juvenile fiction. I. Fernandez, Laura II. Jacobson, Rick III. Title.

PS8555.O887V58 2004   jC813'.6   C2003-901067-8
                             PZ7

6 5 4 3 2 1   Printed and bound in Canada   04 05 06 07 08

To my sons, John and Aidan,
in fond recollection of hot chocolate in St. Mark's Square.

D.C.C.

This book is dedicated to Enrique Fernandez
who loved music and instilled that love in all of us.

A special thank-you to Mor, our underpainter, whose help made
the completion of this book possible, and to Ulysses, our Venetian gondolier,
who showed us a Venice from another time.

L.F. & R.J.

"Ahoy, ahoy! Venice, the Queen of the Sea!"

Katarina rushed to the ship's railing and looked out over the splashing waves.

She couldn't believe her eyes. A magic island was coming closer and closer. Sunlight danced and flashed on its golden towers and domes.

Venice! The city was like the crown of a queen, a queen rising from the blue waters of the sea.

But there were more surprises.

$\mathcal{T}$he whole city seemed to have gone mad!

Musicians sang "Long live Carnival!" as Katarina arrived on the dock. Jugglers tossed candy balls. High above, a tumbler somersaulted across a high wire.

"Why is everyone wearing a mask?" Katarina asked a gondolier.

The young man laughed and gave her a mask to wear. "Everyone wears a mask during Carnival, Signorina. A rich man can pretend to be a beggar, and a beggar can be a rich man!"

The gondolier introduced himself as Giovanni and helped Katarina into his gondola.

"Can you take me to the School of the Pietà, Giovanni?" she asked.

He looked at her closely. "That's the school for the orphans, isn't it?"

$\mathscr{K}$atarina blushed behind her mask and hugged her violin case tightly.

Yes, she was an orphan. She had grown up with the nuns in the hills of Cremona. They had taught her how to play the violin. When the music surrounded her, she forgot the lonely nights without a mother or father to tuck her in.

And now she was travelling to a new school, a school where she would be with other students who loved music.

Giovanni poled his gondola through the back canals of Venice, away from the laughter of Carnival. He stopped at the school. It looked more like a prison.

Katarina knocked and the great door swung open. Her life was about to change.

$\mathcal{T}$he cold marble floors made her shiver as she walked along the dark corridor. Then she heard something, faintly at first, but growing louder and louder. Katarina ran to the last door in the hall and opened it.

Music! She had never heard such wonderful music. And all of the musicians were girls! Violins, cellos, trumpets, oboes — all played by girls!

Standing before them, a man with fiery red hair nodded his head in time to the music. Then he raised his violin and began to play. The instrument seemed to sing in his hands. The music was everywhere — in her ears, in her head . . . in her heart.

Katarina realized that it could be none other than the famous composer Antonio Vivaldi!

"Look, the new girl!" a voice called out.

The music stopped and everyone turned to stare at Katarina.

"Come up here, my dear," Don Antonio called out. "What is your name?"

Katarina walked to the front of the class. "My name is Katarina." She looked down and blushed. "I don't have another name."

Don Antonio smiled and pointed to the girls in the class. "All of the girls here are orphans, so we give them the names of their instruments. Here's Giulietta the Guitar and Susanna the Flute."

A girl called out from the back, "Some people say it's unladylike for girls to play bassoons and trombones; they're only for boys. But we play everything — even the timpani!"

She gave the drum a loud wallop and everyone laughed — even Katarina.

"Now, girls," Don Antonio said. "I have some intriguing news for you."

"*T*omorrow is our Grand Concert for Carnival, and we have a special guest — the Duke of Cremona. He has sent us a rather mysterious gift. Come over here."

The curious girls gathered around the table, on which lay a beautiful violin case. It was decorated with a picture of a nightingale. The diamonds in its eyes seemed to flash just for Katarina. She fingered the ring on a chain around her neck. It, too, had a nightingale on it.

Don Antonio opened the case. "There's a very sad story attached to this violin. The Duke's son took his wife and child on a sea voyage. A great storm blew the ship onto the rocks. The Duke's son and his wife were drowned."

"What about the child?" asked Katarina.

"No one knows what happened to her, but the Duke is convinced she is still alive," Don Antonio continued. "So he went to the famous violin maker, Signor Stradivarius, and asked him to build a violin with the most beautiful sound in the world — so beautiful, so magical that it could call his grandchild back from the mists."

He paused, picked up the violin and drew his bow across the strings. Katarina closed her eyes. The note seemed to hover in the rafters high above.

"Each year the Duke asks someone new to play the violin and call the lost child. This year, it is our turn. When the clock strikes midnight on the last night of Carnival, we will all unmask and perhaps — just perhaps — the lost child will appear."

A bell began to ring in the distance.

"But enough of sad stories," Don Antonio said with a chuckle. "There's the bell for lunch. And I think there may be whipped cream on our dessert."

Katarina stayed behind as the girls and Don Antonio disappeared toward the dining hall. She was drawn back irresistibly to the violin. Light fell through the elegant sound holes and illuminated tiny words painted inside.

A poem!

The nightingale takes wing,
Her secret song to sing.

Katarina lifted the violin from its velvet-lined case. Her hands trembled. How it happened she could never tell, but in a moment, the precious instrument had slipped through her fingers and lay broken on the marble floor.

"Oh, no!" Katarina cried out and knelt to gather up the pieces of the violin. "What am I going to do?"

Suddenly, she heard a voice singing outside on the canal.

"Come to your window,
O my beloved,
Open your heart to me,
O hear my song."

Katarina ran to the window. There was Giovanni in his gondola.

"Giovanni, help me!" Katarina cried. She grabbed the broken instrument and its case, and climbed down into his boat.

After she told him what had happened, Giovanni smiled. "Don't worry. I know someone who can help!"

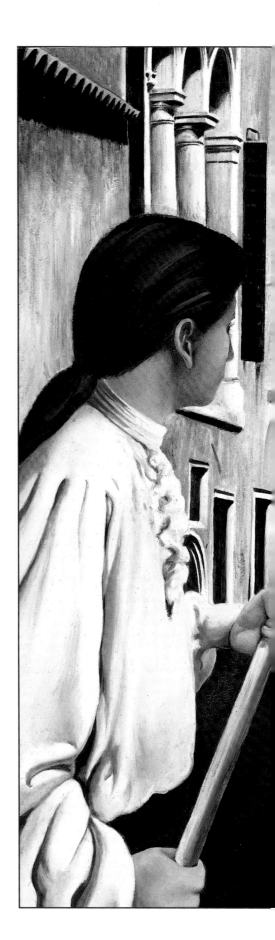

"Where are we going?" Katarina asked anxiously as they left the school behind.

"To the violin maker in St. Mark's Square. During Carnival, everything happens in the square. Tonight they're having fireworks and horse races!"

A rich gondola sailed by, decorated with golden banners and filled with musicians.

"That's the Duke of Cremona's boat!" Giovanni called out.

Katarina held the violin case close. What would happen if the Duke found out about his beautiful violin?

"Here we are! Welcome to the drawing room of Europe!"

Giovanni held the gondola steady as Katarina jumped out and looked in wonder at the great piazza.

An old woman tapped her shoulder. "Sweets, my sweet?"

Her basket was filled with chocolates. Katarina nodded gratefully and chose a heart-shaped one.

"Look out!" Giovanni called.

An egg flew through the air and exploded beside Katarina. In the distance, a masked boy laughed and reached for another.

Katarina sniffed. "They're filled with perfume."

"It means he likes you! Run!"

Katarina laughed and nimbly dodged the eggs. In the shadows of the arcade, a man in black watched in silence.

$\mathcal{K}$atarina and Giovanni were still laughing when they ran into the violin maker's little shop under the bell tower.

"Children, children," he said, "adagio not allegro!"

Katarina showed him the broken violin.

The old man's eyes widened in surprise. "But this is a Stradivarius!" he whispered. "One of the finest violins in the world."

Katarina's desperation returned. "You must fix it," she pleaded.

"Come back tomorrow," the old man said, and disappeared into his workshop.

No one noticed the face at the window.

$\mathcal{K}$atarina said nothing as Giovanni took her back to the school.

For the rest of the day, she couldn't concentrate on her work. Even in music class, her fingers just didn't want to play. All she could think about was the broken violin. Would it be fixed in time for the Grand Concert? Would Don Antonio notice it was missing?

At the same time, a deeper question began to awake inside of her. Was there a connection between the violin's nightingale and the one on her ring?

"*K*atarina!"

That night a hoarse whisper sounded below Katarina's window. She jumped in fright and ran to open the shutters.

"Giovanni . . . is that you?" she called into the darkness.

"Yes, Katarina. I went back to the violin maker. He said that a man dressed all in black came and took the violin." Giovanni sounded scared.

"He stole it?" Katarina was frantic.

"He left this letter." Giovanni pulled out a piece of paper.

Katarina climbed down into the gondola and took the paper from him. "Look, there's a nightingale on the seal! And inside, another poem . . .

Come follow me this night;
My grave will give you light," she read.

"What could that mean?" Katarina puzzled.

"It can be only one thing," Giovanni replied. "I know a place. It's kind of scary, but it might solve this mystery."

"Please take me there!" Katarina told him.

They glided off into the night, the moon shining cold and pale on the water. Masked dancers drifted across the bridges like ghosts, but the canals were silent and dark.

Katarina saw something move. "Giovanni, I think someone is following us!" she cried out.

"Where?" Giovanni asked.

"He's . . . he's gone!" Katarina replied, looking around at the darkened windows and passageways. She shivered.

A raven called out in warning as Giovanni brought the gondola up beside a crumbling wooden dock. "Welcome to the Island of the Dead, Signorina," he said in his best spooky voice.

"What are we doing in a cemetery?" Katarina asked as they made their way along a row of old tombs. A cold wind began to blow, and thunder rumbled in the distance.

"The poem mentioned a grave, and I remember seeing a nightingale on one of the tombs here. Here it is." Giovanni held up the lantern.

Katarina ran her hand across the inscription carved on the tomb. "Here's the poem! Look, there are more lines," she exclaimed, and read aloud,

"Await the midnight song;
The truth will come ere long."

Katarina grabbed Giovanni's lantern and held it high.

"What are you looking for?" he asked.

"A name . . . anything. Help me!" she cried.

Suddenly, a flash of lightning tore across the sky. Thunder seemed to shake the tombs. Giovanni and Katarina ran to the gondola and launched out into the waves just as the rain began to fall.

*K*atarina was soaked when she climbed back through the school's window. But she was not shivering from the cold. She was frightened.

Was the man in black following them? Why had he sent them to that tomb?

She looked around the hall. Garlands of flowers and tapestries hung from all the walls. Everything and everyone was ready for the Grand Concert the next day.

Everyone except her. She was all alone. Katarina fingered the nightingale ring on its chain. "Oh, nightingale," she whispered. "Bring me luck tomorrow."

And she slipped silently down the corridor to her bed.

$\mathcal{T}$he next morning the school bell rang out over the courtyard for the last day of Carnival. The girls ran to the fountain to admire their concert dresses.

"How do these flowers look in my hair?" asked Rosa.

"Like seaweed," Maria snorted. "Here, let me fix them."

Katarina looked around. "Where's Don Antonio?" she asked.

No one knew. He had disappeared.

"But who will play the concerto for the Duke?" Katarina wondered.

A voice called out from the balcony. "Hurry up, the guests are starting to arrive!"

All the gondolas of Venice seemed to turn toward the doors of the school that evening. The light of a thousand torches and lanterns lit up every window and doorway, scattering reflections like diamonds across the waters.

Great ladies floated up the steps in rich silks, while young poets strained their necks to find a new sweetheart.

Then the Duke's splendid gondola came along the canal, pulling up right next to Giovanni's. The Duke wore a mask, but his eyes were blue, as blue as the waves of the sea. And always searching. Searching for something . . . someone.

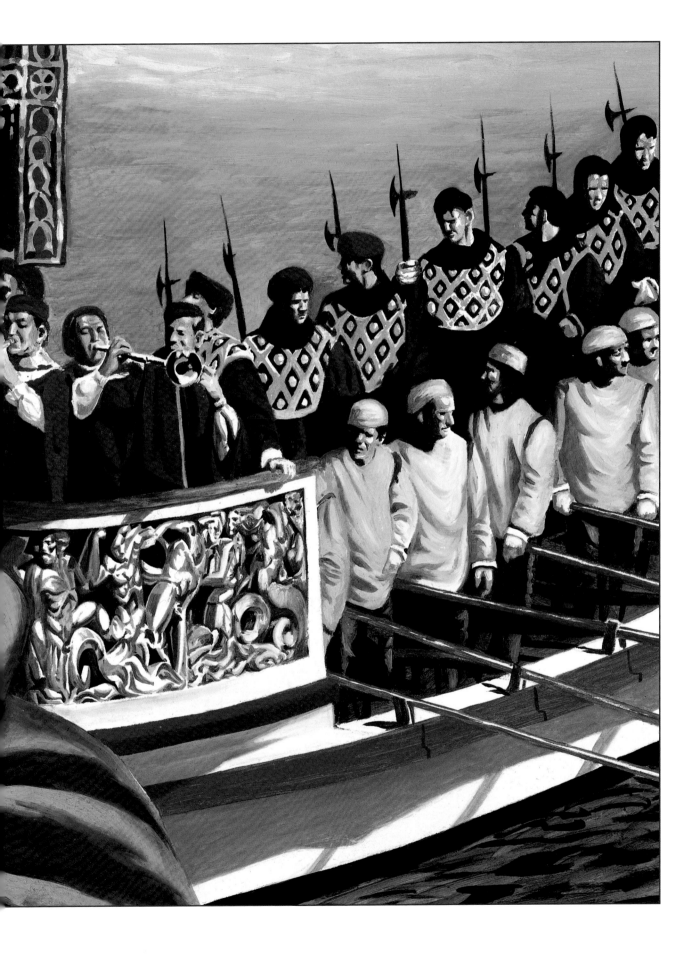

All the great gentlemen and ladies bowed and curtsied as the Duke passed through the door and into the hall where the girls were waiting to play.

But where was Don Antonio?

The girls looked at each other in panic. Who was going to play the concerto?

The midnight bell began to chime. The Duke raised his hand for the music to begin. Somehow the girls began to play.

And then, in the distance, a violin began to sing.

The doors opened, and down the aisle came a mysterious man in black. In his hands was the Duke's violin, and he was playing as no one had ever played before.

The music called to Katarina. As if in a dream, she stood and found herself walking through the rows of the orchestra until her eyes met the Duke's. He removed his mask. And from deep inside her, from a place that only music could reach, a name floated to her lips:

"Grandfather!"

Tears rolled down the old man's face. Katarina took the violin from the man in black. Her bow rose and fell across the strings like the lullaby of gentle waves.

$\mathcal{A}$s she finished playing, the man in black spoke at last.

"The nightingale takes wing,
Her secret song to sing."

Then he removed his mask.

"Don Antonio! It was you. You knew all the time!" Katarina laughed in relief.

Don Antonio chuckled. "I knew from the moment I saw your ring. But you had to find your own self, here in the music. And now your secret song is finished."

The Duke took his granddaughter's hand and led her to his gondola. Passing, Katarina bent down to kiss Giovanni on the cheek.

"Goodbye, my Lady," Giovanni whispered. "Don't ever forget Venice."

As the gondola moved out onto the canal, Katarina turned and waved one last time to Don Antonio.

The sun was rising, golden above the waves of the sea.